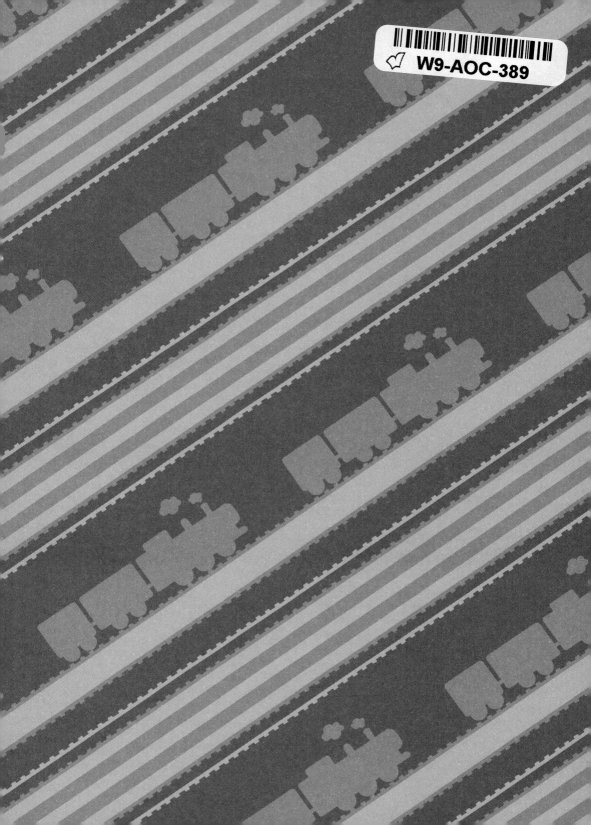

Thomas the Tank Engine & Friends®

A BRITT ALLCROFT COMPANY PRODUCTION

Based on The Railway Series by The Reverend W Awdry

© 2005 Gullane (Thomas) LLC

Thomas the Tank Engine & Friends and Thomas & Friends
are trademarks of Gullane Entertainment Inc.
Thomas the Tank Engine & Friends is Reg. U.S. Pat. TM Off.

A HIT Entertainment Company

www.randomhouse.com/kids/thomas   www.thomasthetankengine.com

Library of Congress Cataloging-in-Publication Data
Go, train, go! : a Thomas the Tank Engine story / illustrated by Tommy Stubbs. — 1st ed.
p. cm. "Thomas the Tank Engine & friends."
Based on The railway series by the Rev. W. Awdry.
"Beginner books."
"A Britt Allcroft Company production."
SUMMARY: Easy-to-read, lyrical text tells how cautious Thomas gives a ride
to a judge who is in a big hurry to get to a train show.
ISBN 0-375-83177-0 (trade) — ISBN 0-375-93177-5 (lib. bdg.)
[1. Railroads—Trains—Fiction.] I. Stubbs, Tommy, ill. II. Awdry, W.
PZ7.A9613Gn 2005   [E]—dc22   2004020062

Printed in the United States of America   First Edition   10 9 8 7 6 5 4 3 2 1

Go, Train, Go!

A Thomas the Tank Engine Story

Based on *The Railway Series*
by The Reverend W Awdry

Illustrated by Tommy Stubbs

BEGINNER BOOKS® A Division of Random House, Inc.

Here comes the judge
in her big red hat.
She has come to see the train show.
Who will take the judge to the train show?

Thomas will!

Thomas will go.

Thomas will take the judge to the show.

"Hurry, Thomas! Take me to the show.
Take me there fast. Go, train, go!"
Clickety-clack, clickety-clack,
up, up the hill,
Thomas the Tank Engine
goes faster than fast.

Screech! go the brakes.

Thomas goes so slow.

Slow,

slow,

slower

than slow he goes.

"Hurry, Thomas! Why do you go so slow?

Take me to the train show. Go, train, go!"

But Thomas cannot go.

Thomas sees a goat.

The goat is on the track.

Peep! Peep! goes Thomas.
Baaaa! The goat jumps back.

Clickety-clack, clickety-clack,
down, down the hill,
Thomas the Tank Engine
goes faster than fast.

Screech! go the brakes.

Thomas goes so slow.

Slow,

slow,

slower

than slow he goes.

"Hurry, Thomas! Why do you go so slow?
Take me to the train show. Go, train, go!"

The tunnel is so dark.

Slow, slow, slow

he goes

into the dark,

       dark,

           dark

               tunnel . . .

. . . and out the other side!

Clickety-clack, clickety-clack,
over a bridge.
He was going so fast.

He was going so fast,
the judge lost her hat!

Screech! go the brakes.

Thomas goes slow.

Slow,

slow,

slow

he goes.

"Hurry, Thomas!
We're running late, you know.
Take me to the train show.
Go, train, go!"

But Thomas must go slow.

There is a cow on the track.

Moo! Moo! goes the cow.

Peep! Peep! goes Thomas.

The cow moves back.

Clickety-clack, clickety-clack,

Thomas the Tank Engine

moves faster than fast!

Screech! go the brakes.

Thomas goes slow.

Slow,

slow,

slow

he goes.

"Don't stop, Thomas. Go, train, go!
Don't stop now. I'm late for the show!"

But Thomas must go slow.

There are logs on the track.

The crane engine clears the logs.
Clickety-clack, clickety-clack,
around the logs goes Thomas
faster than fast.

There is mud up ahead!

The judge wants to go slow.

"Slow, little engine.
Slow, slow, slow.
Watch out for the mud!
Whoa, train, whoa!"

But Thomas cannot go slow.

Thomas goes faster than fast.

Into the mud . . .

Splish! Splash!

Thomas goes fast.

Past a town,

fast, fast.

Past a dog,

faster still.

Fast at last!

Nothing can stop him,
nothing at all.
No goat.
No dark.

No cow.

No log.

No crane.

No mud.

No town.

No dog.

This is the fastest

that Thomas can go!

Screech! go the brakes.

"Good job, Thomas!
We made it here at last!
You are a little engine,
but you go so fast!"

Here comes the judge!

The train show begins.

There are red trains and blue trains
and old trains and new trains.
And a little blue engine covered in mud.
What will the judge say?

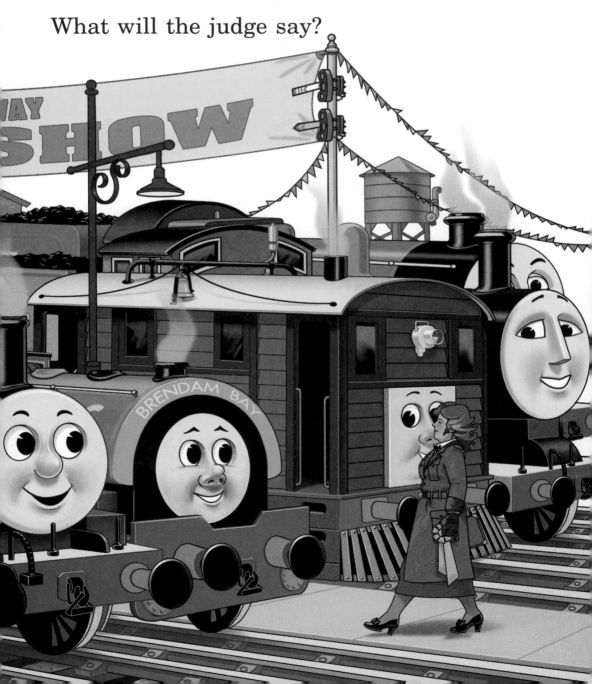

"I like all the trains. You all are such fun. But the muddy little blue train is my favorite one."